the Apple Trees of TSCHLIN

STORY BY G. M. KEARNEY

ILLUSTRATIONS BY REBECCA MILLER

ISBN 13: 978-1-59955-098-5

Published by CFI, an imprint of Cedar Fort, Inc.
2373 W. 700 S., Springville, UT 84663
Distributed by Cedar Fort, Inc., www.cedarfort.com

LIBRARY OF CONGRESS CATALOGING-IN-PUBLICATION DATA

Kearney, G. M. (Gregory Michael), 1957–
  The apple trees of Tschlin / G.M. Kearney.
    p. cm.
  Summary: With the help of three magical apple tree seedlings, the rightful
heir to the kindgom of Tschlin is selected from among the king's three
daughters.
  ISBN 978-1-59955-098-5
  [1. Fairy tales. 2. Princesses—Fiction.] I. Title.
  PZ8.K3Ap 2008
  [E]—dc22
                      2007045101

Jacket design by Nicole Williams
Book design by Angela D. Olsen
Edited by Annaliese B. Cox
Cover design © 2008 by Lyle Mortimer

Printed on acid-free paper

Printed in Hong Kong

10 9 8 7 6 5 4 3 2 1

Dedication

To my daughter Shannon. May all the apples of your life
be sweet and delicious; and to my dear wife, Tamara,
who I love more than words can convey.

The tiny kingdom of Tschlin is a clean and orderly nation. Tucked between Switzerland, Italy, and Austria, most maps do not even show the kingdom or its only town, Villapin. Today, just as in years past, the kingdom of Tschlin remains little more than a hard question on a geography test. But many years ago the kingdom of Tschlin faced a crisis. It is in that crisis and how it was faced that our story is told.

King Wilhelm the First was a good and wise man. He ruled his kingdom with a fair hand and always with the best interest of his subjects at heart. He was rewarded with the loyalty and genuine love of his people. The kingdom of Tschlin was orderly, peaceful, and prosperous under his reign.

There was but a single issue that marred this otherwise tranquil situation: King Wilhelm lacked a son to be his heir to the throne. He did have three bright and beautiful daughters: Princess Erika, who was ten years old; Princess Anna, who was eight; and the youngest, Princess Emma, who was five. Now today we wouldn't think this a problem at all, for surely any one of the princesses would make a fine queen. However, when our story takes place, such a thing was not permitted. As the Archbishop of Villapin would remind the king each Sunday at Mass, both tradition and Tschlin law required that the monarch be male, and, as there were simply no boys in the king's family, this presented a crisis to the small nation.

King Wilhelm and his wife, Queen Emily, had tried to reason with the archbishop, but to no avail. They told him that one of the princesses could rule. The archbishop insisted, however, that only a male heir or a direct sign from God revealing that one of the princesses could rule would change his mind, and the law. It didn't help matters any that the archbishop refused to say what sort of sign from God would permit one of the princesses to rule. So it was that the king faced a dilemma, until one bright spring morning when a monk came into Villapin.

The monk pushed a small cart before him. In the cart were three young trees, each in a pot of dirt. The monk pushed the cart up the hill to the gates of the palace, where he pulled on the rope that rang a bell at the guardhouse. At once the gate was opened and the guard inquired of the monk as to the nature of his business. The monk replied that he had traveled to the palace with gifts for the princesses and an offer to help with the problem that had so vexed the family. Word of the monk and his offer was passed to the king, who ordered that the monk be brought to him at once. The king also asked his family to attend the meeting, for the monk was the first to ever offer a solution to the problem of the heir to the throne.

The monk had the three young trees placed before the king and queen. He then explained that he had brought as a gift to the princesses three magical apple tree seedlings. These trees would, when the time was right, give the royal family an indication as to which princess should be heir to the throne. Each princess was to care for her tree, prune it, and tend to it. However, she must never eat the apples that it produced. For to do so would mean that she was no longer worthy of the throne. The monk assured the king that if the princesses would follow these instructions, the time would come that a tree would give a sign showing which princess should be heir to the kingdom.

With that, he presented each of the princesses with her young apple tree. To Princess Erika, the eldest, he gave the biggest and most developed of the trees. Next was Princess Anna, whose tree, while not as big as her sister's, was still a healthy tree, ready to be planted. To little Princess Emma went the smallest of the trees, barely even a twig. The monk then reminded the girls that each of their trees was magical and that they must care for them well—and under no conditions were they to eat the apples that might grow. He then bowed to the king and queen, thanked them for their kindness in the matter, and left the castle.

The trees were planted, each outside the balconies of the princesses' rooms in the palace. For many years each princess tended to her tree with care. The trees grew and became a most delightful addition to the palace grounds. Many people came to admire the trees and wonder about what sign the trees might give as an indication to which princess should rule over the nation.

About eight years went by, and in that time Princess Erika became dissatisfied with her life in the tiny kingdom. She longed, as many do at her age, to go out and see the world that lay beyond her mountainous home. To enjoy what the cities of Vienna, Paris, and London might have to offer. To meet others of her age who she had not been brought up with.

So Princess Erika left Tschlin and went out into the world. At first the royal gardeners took care of her apple tree, for the family fully expected Erika to return home someday. As the years went by, reports of Princess Erika's wild behavior became more common in the palace, and the tree—which had once been the most beautiful of the three—began to wither and die.

Nothing the gardeners did seemed to stop the decay. And then one winter's night in a storm the tree was blown over. So ended any hope of Princess Erika ascending to the throne.

Princess Anna had been more obedient in caring for her tree, and in her sixteenth year the tree gave fruit. It was in that year that the first of many suitors came to call at the palace. Each sought the interest of Anna, who had grown into a young woman of exceptional beauty, with a quick wit and a beguiling smile. Many in the kingdom came to believe that Anna would someday rule over them, for she seemed to possess every talent and attribute of her father.

One day a young man appeared in the kingdom. Like so many others before him, he too took a liking to the young princess. Only this time the feeling seemed to be mutual. He was handsome and sophisticated and spoke of the many lands and cities that he had visited in his travels. He told Anna that she would accompany him on his travels to far-off kingdoms. To meet presidents, princes, and potentates. To see the Great Wall of China and the gardens of Baghdad.

Anna was smitten, and one day as she sat with him under her apple tree, hearing again of the places they might visit, the young man reached up an picked an apple from the tree. Before Anna could protest, he had taken a bite of the apple.

"What have you done!" she cried. She then explained about the tree and the promise she had made never to eat from it. The young man laughed. What foolishness, he had said. Why, apples had been placed on the earth to enjoy, not to be left on the tree to rot away like the leaves in the fall. The more she thought about this the more convinced Anna became that the young man was right. She too took a bite of the apple, but it did not have the sweet taste that she had expected. Rather, when she looked she saw that the apple was filled with worms. She had been lured into eating the apple by a man who had made many promises of adventure, but, in fact, had delivered none of them.

Anna grew sad as she realized what she had done and what she had given up in a moment of weakness. Soon she too left to join her elder sister in the cities of Europe. Her mother and father grieved the loss of yet another daughter.

Emma had always been the daughter overlooked by others. Where her older sisters had been the center of attention, Emma had always seemed to be the princess that the people of the kingdom forgot: The "other princess," as she was often referred to.

Over the years she had cared with devotion for the tree that had been given to her—even though it was small and only occasionally bore fruit. In this task she had always had the help of Anthony, the son and apprentice of the printer. He was Emma's only close friend. He was now a lanky printer's assistant with the ink-stained hands of a craftsman. Together they had tended the tree for these many years, and together they had watched as it had grown from a twig to a modest-sized tree.

In all that time it had delivered very few apples. Emma and Anthony were careful never to handle the apples, for fear they might be tempted to eat one. The tree had stood outside Emma's balcony, having grown only as high as the balcony from which Emma had watched as carriages carried away her sisters to lands and adventures unknown to her.

As Emma grew older, there were, from time to time, suitors—but Emma found all these young men to be dull and uninteresting. Most, it seemed, had their eyes more on the kingdom of Tschlin and less on the young princess with the piercing blue eyes. One day after a particularly frustrating meeting with one of these suitors, she stormed out into the garden and collapsed in tears under her apple tree. After what seemed ages, she heard Anthony's familiar voice.

"Emma?" said the cautious voice, not wishing to make matters worse. Emma looked up to see her childhood friend looking down at her. "What's the matter?" he asked, offering his hand to help her up.

As they walked around the garden, Emma explained her troubles to the young printer. How she felt the world on her shoulders as she tried to make the right decision. How the loss of her sisters had only made matters worse for her. How the decisions about her life affected not only her but her nation as well. And finally, how she wished that the tree would somehow give the sign that the whole kingdom was waiting for.

Anthony listened as Emma wept over her predicament and that of her family. After a long pause he spoke. "Emma, would you marry me?" he asked in a voice so shy that at first Emma didn't believe what she had heard. Emma looked at Anthony and nodded her head in agreement. As she did so, a warm breeze blew a rain of white blossoms down upon them. They looked up to see that the tree, which had only moments ago been bare, was now filled with beautiful blossoms. The tree that had seemed for so long to only show the promise of a bountiful harvest of fruit now spread forth a vast white canopy of blossoms. In but an instant it had been transformed from the least of the three trees to the most magnificent.

"The sign!" Emma exclaimed, and so it was.

Emma and Anthony were married that summer in the cathedral in Villapin, and as the happy couple emerged from the church with the bells pealing overhead in joyous celebration of the marriage of the princess and the printer, an old monk approached and placed an apple in Emma's hand. "You have lived well and true, my dear, and now you are free to eat of the fruit of the tree I gave to you." Before Emma could thank him, the monk once more disappeared into the crowd of her subjects.

The apple that he gave her that day was sweet and delicious, as were all the apples that the tree produced each year from then on.

The End